For Molly Belle —P.M.

In loving memory of
my grandmothers, Mildred
and Gladys —D.M.

© 2016 by Pamela Mayer
Illustrations copyright © 2016 Deborah Melmon

KAR-BEN PUBLISHING, INC.
A division of Lerner Publishing Group, Inc.
241 First Avenue North
Minneapolis, MN 55401 USA
1-800-4-KARBEN

Website address: www.karben.com

Main body text set in Chauncy Decaf Medium 18/23
Typeface provided by Chank

Library of Congress Cataloging-in-Publication Data

Names: Mayer, Pamela, author. | Melmon, Deborah, illustrator.
Title: Chicken soup, chicken soup / by Pamela Mayer ; illustrated by Deborah Melmon.
Description: Minneapolis : Kar-Ben Publishing, [2016] | Summary: "Two grandmas. Two delicious recipes. Sophie loves Bubbe's Jewish chicken soup, made with kreplach. She also loves Nai Nai's Chinese chicken soup, with wonton. But don't tell Bubbe and Nai Nai that their soups are the same!"— Provided by publisher.
Identifiers: LCCN 2015040981 (print) | LCCN 2016005013 (ebook) | ISBN 9781467789349 (lb : alk. paper) | ISBN 9781467794145 (pb : alk. paper) | ISBN 9781512409420 (eb pdf)
Subjects: | CYAC: Grandmothers—Fiction. | Soups—Fiction. | Jews—United States—Fiction. | Chinese Americans—Fiction. | Racially mixed people—Fiction.
Classification: LCC PZ7.M463 Ch 2016 (print) | LCC PZ7.M463 (ebook) | DDC [E]—dc23
LC record available at http://lccn.loc.gov/2015040981

PJ Library Edition ISBN 978-1-5124-0840-9
Manufactured in China
2-49192-21213-3/23/2020
102034K2/B0908/A6

CHICKEN SOUP, CHICKEN SOUP

Pamela Mayer

Illustrated by Deborah Melmon

KAR-BEN
PUBLISHING

Two grandmas.

Two soup pots.

Two family traditions.

Two recipes for chicken soup?

Uh-oh . . .

How could a little piece of dough, stuffed with meat and floating in a bowl of chicken soup, cause a problem?

It started one rainy afternoon when I went to my bubbe's—my Grandma Ellie's—for lunch.

"Sophie, darling, here's a nice bowl of hot chicken soup for you."

I picked up my spoon and smiled when I saw the dumpling in my soup. "Yum! Wonton—my favorite!"

"Wonton? Who's a wonton?" Bubbe asked.

"Silly Bubbe—in the soup!"

"Sophie, *my zissele*, *my sweet one*, those are kreplach, not wontons. This is Jewish chicken soup, which I make for you just the way my bubbe made it for me. Now eat — it's delicious."

For the rest of the afternoon we played dress-up and had a wonderful time.

But when Mommy came to pick me up I heard Bubbe muttering about a granddaughter who didn't know the difference between kreplach and wontons.

A few days later I went to my *nai nai's*—my Grandma Nancy's—for lunch.

"Here you are, Sophie, good hot soup," Nai Nai said.

"Mmmm, kreplach," I said. "I love kreplach."

"What's kreplach?" Nai Nai asked.

"Silly Nai Nai—in the soup."

"Sophie, my *baobao*, my baby, my treasure, this is Chinese chicken soup with wonton. I make it for you, just the way my nai nai made it for me. Now eat and grow strong."

For the rest of the afternoon nai nai and I had fun painting pictures.

But when Daddy came to pick me up, I heard her talking to him about a granddaughter who didn't know the difference between wontons and kreplach.

I knew the difference between soup with kreplach and soup with wontons! I just accidentally mixed them up. Bubbe's chicken soup had carrots and parsley. Nai Nai's chicken soup had bamboo shoots and green onions. Wontons are not kreplach. Kreplach are not wontons.

Carrots

Parsley

Bamboo Shoots

Green onion

Kreplach

Wontons

A little different.

A lot the same.

And I could prove it.

When I told Mommy and Daddy about my idea, they liked it. So the next week, I invited Bubbe and Nai Nai to our house for lunch. I asked each of them to bring their soup.

Soon Bubbe's chicken soup with kreplach simmered on the stove next to Nai Nai's chicken soup with wontons.

"Your soup smells very good, Nancy," Bubbe said.

"Yours too, Ellie," Nai Nai said.

I took a big serving bowl out of the drawer.

Daddy helped me pour in both soups until the two were mixed together.

"Presenting the first ever Jewish Chinese Kreplach Wonton Chicken Soup!" I said.

Mommy ladled the new soup into bowls and we all sat down at the table.

"You know," Bubbe said, "to be completely honest, my chicken soup isn't exactly the way my bubbe made it. I buy wonton wrappers to make my kreplach."

"So your Jewish chicken soup is a little bit Chinese?" I asked.

Bubbe nodded. "That's right."

"I have something to say too," Nai Nai said. "I buy the chicken for my soup at the kosher market. The flavor is better."

"So your Chinese chicken soup is a little bit Jewish?" I asked.

"Yes, it is," Nai Nai said.

"A little Jewish, a little Chinese—a lot like me," I said.

"Sophie Chang, you're a genius," Bubbe said.

"I've always thought so," Nai Nai agreed.

"Kreplach schmeplach, let's eat," Bubbe said.

"Wait a minute, don't you mean wonton schmonton?" nai nai asked.

I laughed and dipped my spoon into my bowl.

A bite of kreplach, a taste of wontons. "Mmmm," I said.

Mommy, Daddy, Bubbe and nai nai all started eating.

"A wonderful blend," Bubbe said.

"The best of both," said nai nai, "just like our granddaughter."

Suddenly I knew what made Bubbe's and nai nai's soups so much alike!
The special ingredient in every bowl of any grandma's soup is love.

"Save room, everybody," Bubbe said. "I made knishes."

"And I brought egg roll," Nai Nai said.

"Are we talking dough filled with vegetables, then fried?" Bubbe asked.

"Precisely," Nai Nai said.

I couldn't wait to taste my first eggknish—or kneggroll.
I knew it would be delicious.

Bubbe and Nai Nai's Chicken Soup

4 pounds (1800 g) chicken
12 cups (3 L) cold water
1 onion, sliced
1 carrot, sliced

2 tsp. salt
1 bay leaf
2 sprigs parsley

Clean the chicken and place it in a large pot. Cover the chicken with cold water. Add the onion, carrot, salt, bay leaf, and parsley. Bring to a boil, then simmer for 3 hours. Remove the chicken, vegetables, bay leaf, and parsley and skim off the fat. (Green onions, carrots, and other vegetables may be added or substituted according to the preference of the "chef.") Always be sure to have a grown-up help when using knives or the stove!

Bubbe's Kreplach (with thanks to the author's bubbe, Manya Pavlovsky)

1 Tbsp. canola oil

1/2 cup (8 Tbsp.) finely chopped onion

4 finely chopped chicken livers

1 tsp. kosher salt

¼ tsp. black pepper

1 48-piece package wonton wrappers (use as many as needed)

Heat the oil in a small skillet and cook the onions until soft, about 3 minutes. Add the chicken liver and continue to cook until browned. Add the salt and pepper. Remove from the heat and let the mixture cool.

Use two wonton wrappers for each kreplach. Wet one wrapper with water around the edges (a fingertip works well for this), and place the other wrapper on top. Spoon a teaspoon of the filling into the center of the wonton wrappers. Fold diagonally to make a triangle, making sure to press out any air. Roll or crimp the edges, using more water to make a tight seal. Continue until the filling is used up.

Drop into a pot of hot chicken soup and cook about 5 minutes.

Nai Nai's Wontons (with thanks to Anna Cao for the recipe of her mother, Jie Rong Zhou)

1 pound (450 g) ground chicken

4 finely chopped water chestnuts

1 tablespoon grated ginger

1/4 cup (4 Tbsp.) finely chopped cilantro

1/4 cup (4 Tbsp.) finely chopped green onion, white parts only

2 Tbsp. soy sauce

1 tsp. canola oil

1 tsp. salt

1 48-piece package wonton wrappers (use as many as needed)

Mix the ground chicken with water chestnuts, ginger, cilantro, green onion, soy sauce, oil and salt. Lay one wonton wrapper on your left hand so it looks like a triangle. Place a teaspoon of the filling on the corner edge. Fold the wonton wrapper 2 times over the filling to make a triangle. Moisten the corners with water. Bring the two ends together so they overlap. Press to seal. Repeat with remaining wontons.

Bring a large pot of water to boil. Add wontons, and let boil for 5-8 minutes, until they rise to the top. Remove the dumplings with a slotted spoon and place in soup bowls. Pour hot chicken broth over each serving.